Elmo Saves Christmas

Based on the "Sesame Street" TV Special by
Christine Ferraro and Tony Geiss

Illustrated by Ellen Appleby

A Random House PICTUREBACK®

Random House/Children's Television Workshop

On Sesame Street, Maria is played by Sonia Manzano, Luis by Emilio Delgado,
Bob by Bob McGrath, and Mr. Hanford by David Langston Smyrl.
Copyright © 1997 Children's Television Workshop.
Jim Henson's Sesame Street Muppets © 1997 Jim Henson Productions, Inc.
Sesame Street and the Sesame Street sign are trademarks and service marks of Children's Television Workshop.
All rights reserved under International and Pan-American Copyright Conventions.
Published in the United States by Random House, Inc., New York, and simultaneously in Canada by Random
House of Canada Limited, Toronto, in conjunction with Children's Television Workshop.

http://www.randomhouse.com/
http://www.sesamestreet.com
ISBN: 0-679-88765-2
Library of Congress Catalog Card Number: 97-066887
Printed in the United States of America 10 9 8 7 6 5 4 3 2

It all began on a Christmas Eve on Sesame Street.

Everyone was busy getting ready for Christmas. Ernie and
Bert were decorating the tree. Maria and Luis were bringing
presents. And Elmo was hurrying home carrying a plate piled
high with cookies. The cookies were for Santa Claus!

Elmo put out the plate of cookies and a glass of milk for
Santa. Then he hung his stocking by the chimney with care.

Elmo climbed into his comfy chair to wait for Santa.

"This year Elmo will definitely, definitely see Santa Claus come down the chimney and eat the cookies!" he said. "Elmo won't fall asleep like last year. No, no, no!"

But soon Elmo was snoring.

Thump! Bump!

A clunky noise woke Elmo with a start. It was Santa Claus, stuck in the chimney.

"Don't worry, Santa!" Elmo called up the chimney. "Elmo will pull you out!" He grabbed a boot and pulled and pulled until Santa Claus came crashing down into the fireplace with his bag of toys and one little reindeer named Lightning.

"Elmo, you are a furry little hero!" said Santa. "When you pulled me out of that chimney, you saved Christmas for kids all over the world!"

So Santa gave Elmo a very special Christmas present—a magical snow globe—with *three wishes!*

Santa Claus and his reindeer Lightning whisked back up the chimney to finish delivering presents to children around the world. Elmo shook the snow globe until the snow flew, and he made his first wish.

"Elmo is thirsty," he said. "Elmo wishes for . . . a glass of water!"

Zing! A glass of clear water appeared.

"It works!" cried Elmo.

On Christmas morning, Elmo went outside to celebrate with his friends.

"Everybody loves Christmas," he said. He made his second wish. "Elmo wishes that . . . it will be Christmas every day!" And—*zing!*—his wish came true!

The next day at the North Pole, Santa's elves had to go right back to work, and they were not happy.

"It's Christmas again?" wailed Frankie the elf. "It was Christmas yesterday! It's usually only once a year!"

But everyone on Sesame Street was joyful that it was
Christmas again.

"Yay! Elmo got his wish!" they said.

"Christmas again!" cried the Count. "That makes two
wonderful Christmases! Ah-ah-ah!"

When the elves told Santa Claus about Elmo's second wish, he hitched Lightning to the sleigh and flew to Sesame Street to visit Elmo.

"You can't have Christmas every day!" Santa told Elmo.

"Why not?" Elmo asked.

"I'll show you."

Santa put Elmo in the sleigh and sent him off into the future to see for himself what would happen if it were Christmas every day.

First, Lightning took Elmo to see Christmas
in the springtime, when it was warm. Christmas looked different.
"Today makes 96 Christmases in a row!" counted the Count.

Then Lightning took Elmo further into the future to see
Christmas again, in the summer, when it was hot.
"That's 193 Christmases," said the Count. "When will it end?"

Elmo began to wonder if Christmas every day
was making people happy after all.

Elmo asked Lightning to take him still further into the future, to the real Christmas Day—December 25—in the cold winter. Maybe then his friends would be cheerful again.

But everybody on Sesame Street was tired of Christmas, even the Count.

"That's 365 Christmases," said the Count, "and I am tired of counting them! When it is Christmas every day," the Count told his little red chum, "Christmas is no longer special."

"Elmo thought it would make people happy," said Elmo. "But it's making them sad.

"Santa was right. Every day can't be Christmas."

"Hey, everybody, Elmo has great news!" he called to his friends. "Elmo has one more wish, and Elmo's third wish is . . . that everything on Sesame Street will be just like it used to be, when Christmas was only *once* a year!"

Everyone rejoiced. And that is the story of how Elmo saved Christmas.

Oh, Elmo has one more wish.
MERRY CHRISTMAS, EVERYBODY!